T ittle Tiger book belongs to:

____

____

____

For my cousin Helen, with love

~ C F

To my niece, Ella Victoria Wernert

~ T M

LITTLE TIGER PRESS
An imprint of Magi Publications
1 The Coda Centre, 189 Munster Road, London SW6 6AW
www.littletigerpress.com

First published in Great Britain 2007
This edition published 2007

A CIP catalogue record for this book is available from the British Library

• ISBN 978-1-84506-457-0

Printed in China

2 4 6 8 10 9 7 5 3 1

One Magical Day

Claire Freedman   Tina Macnaughton

LITTLE TIGER PRESS
London

Night shadows fade
to a pale, golden dawn.
It's a magical day –
wake up, Little Fawn!

Mother Duck wakens
her brood with a kiss.
This beautiful morning
is too good to miss!

Up in the poppy field
frisky lambs play,
Skipping with joy
at this new summer's day.

Small piglets scamper
and skip in the sun,
Rolling in mud,
having such squelchy fun!

Warm breezes drift
down the flower-filled lanes,
Where fluffy-tailed puppies
chase round, playing games.

Into the stable
the bright sunlight streams,
Bathing the foal
with its soft, golden beams.

Sun-drowsy kittens
pad home to their mother.
Washed one by one,
they curl up with each other.

Happy and free,
the wild swallow weaves,
Then swoops to her nest,
built high in the eaves.

Little calves rest
in the shade of the trees,
Where butterflies dance
on the fresh, gentle breeze.

Donkey nods off
in the last patch of sun.
Softly the light fades,
the day's almost done.

Blinking in wonder,
two shy fox cubs peep,
As deep in the meadow,
the long shadows creep.

Stars shine like diamonds,
the full moon gleams bright,
Gently Owl hoots –
it's a magical night!

More magical reads from Little Tiger Press

I'M NOT GOING OUT THERE!
PAUL BRIGHT
BEN CORT

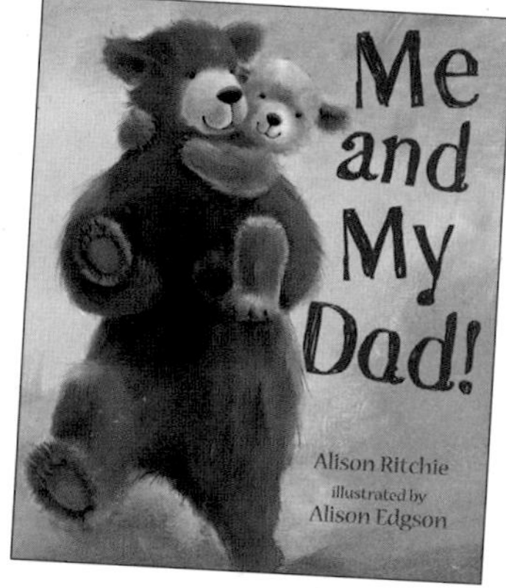
Me and My Dad!
Alison Ritchie
illustrated by
Alison Edgson

cock-a-doodle-
hooooooo!
Mick Manning
Brita Granström

The Most Precious Thing
Gill Lewis
Louise Ho

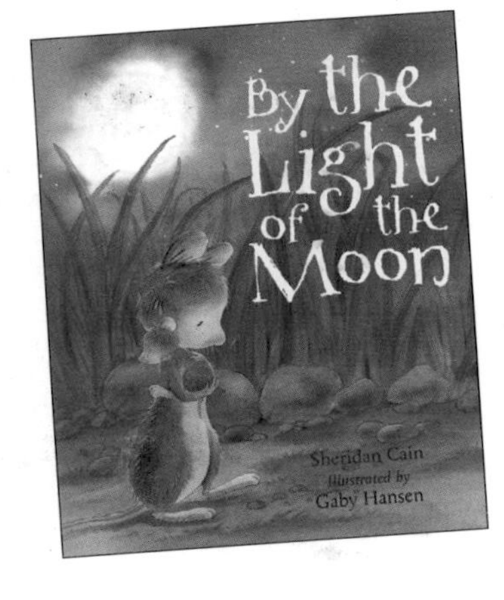
By the Light of the Moon
Sheridan Cain
illustrated by
Gaby Hansen

Snuggle Up, Sleepy Ones
Claire Freedman
illustrated by
Tina Macnaughton

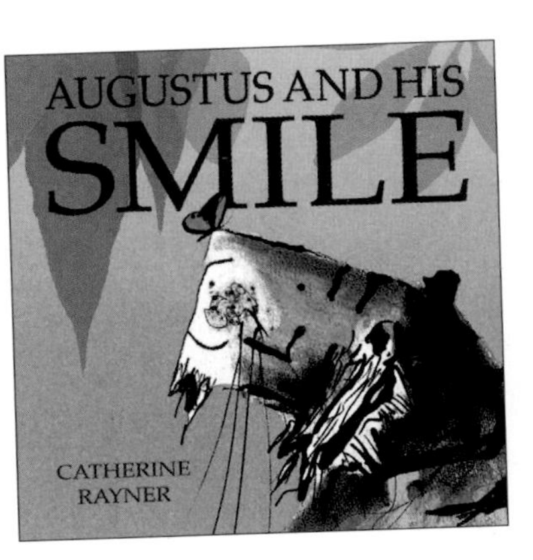
AUGUSTUS AND HIS
SMILE
CATHERINE
RAYNER

For information regarding any of the above titles
or for our catalogue, please contact us:
Little Tiger Press, 1 The Coda Centre,
189 Munster Road, London SW6 6AW
Tel: 020 7385 6333 Fax: 020 7385 7333
E-mail: info@littletiger.co.uk
www.littletigerpress.com